# Grizzly Bears

Written by Michèle Dufresne

PIONEER VALLEY EDUCATIONAL PRESS, INC.

Here is a brown bear.
Brown bears
are called grizzly bears.

3

Grizzly bears can climb trees.

Grizzly bears can swim.

Look at this
grizzly bear's shoulder.
Can you see the hump
on the bear's shoulder?

Shoulder ▼

Here is a grizzly bear eating grass.
They like to eat grass and berries.

Look at this grizzly bear
in the river.
Grizzly bears like to eat fish.

Grizzly bears are omnivorous.
They eat both plants and animals.

11

Grizzly bears sleep in the winter.

Grizzly bears hibernate during the winter for 5-8 months.

They wake up in the spring and look for food.
They are hungry.

Here is a mother
grizzly bear and her cubs.

# Grizzly Bears

grass

shoulder

berries

cubs

grizzly bear